SOMETHING

ONE SMALL THING CAN MAKE A DIFFERENCE

Written by
Natalee Creech

and Illustrated by Pablo Pino

WORTHY
kids™

ISBN: 978-1-5460-0287-1

WorthyKids, Hachette Book Group, 1290 Avenue of the Americas, New York, NY 10104

Library of Congress Cataloging-in-Publication Data

Names: Creech, Natalee, author. | Pino, Pablo, illustrator.
Title: Something / written by Natalee Creech ; illustrated by Pablo Pino.
Description: First edition. | New York : WorthyKids, [2023] | Audience:
  Ages 4-7. | Summary: Encourages children to take whatever action they
  can, no matter how small, to show love to the people around them and
  make the world a better place.
Identifiers: LCCN 2022025063 | ISBN 9781546002871 (hardcover)
Subjects: CYAC: Stories in rhyme. | Compassion—Fiction. |
  Kindness—Fiction. | LCGFT: Stories in rhyme. | Picture books.
Classification: LCC PZ8.3.C86 So 2023 | DDC [E]—dc23
LC record available at https://lccn.loc.gov/2022025063

Designed by Eve DeGrie

Printed and bound in China
WAI
10 9 8 7 6 5 4 3 2

To Grace, who is always doing something for someone. ~N.C.

For Agos and Jesica, may life fill us with moments to share something. ~P.P.

"For I was hungry and you gave me something to eat,
I was thirsty and you gave me something to drink,
I was a stranger and you invited me in,
I needed clothes and you clothed me,
I was sick and you looked after me,
I was in prison and you came to visit me."

—MATTHEW 25:35–36

When I know a friend is hurting,
then my heart starts aching too,

like it's asking me a question . . .

is there SOMETHING I can do?

What you're feeling
is compassion.
It's GOD'S WHISPER
to your heart:
"Will you try to help this person?
Can you find a way to start?"

If there's something that you notice,
there is something you can do.
Keep your KINDNESS RADAR working—
maybe something
starts with YOU!

Do I have to be a grown-up?
I can't even drive a car!

No! Young or old,
we all can help,
whatever age we are!

I can help an older person
water plants or get the mail.

I can carry out the items
for my grandma's rummage sale!

I can try to find forever homes
for each abandoned pet . . .

or come up with a grand invention
no one's thought of yet!

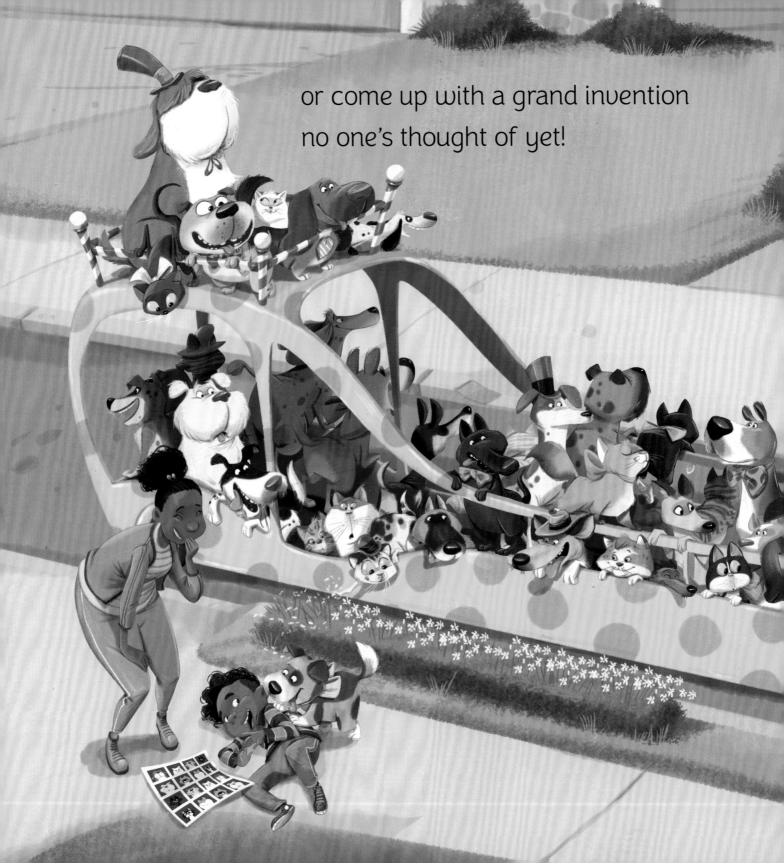

YES!

Your something could be anything
that's helping anyone:
a card, a coat, a "Come on in!",
a hand to get it done!

If there's something that you notice,
there is something you can do.
Keep your KINDNESS RADAR working—
maybe something
starts with YOU!

Do I need a lot of money?
Will I have to buy supplies?

No! You can make a difference with your heart or hands or eyes.

I can help out at
a food bank.

I can plant a
thousand seeds.

I can cultivate a garden
where we all take
what we need.

If my friend is
sick or lonely,
I can help make
chicken soup.

I can welcome my new neighbors and include them in the group.

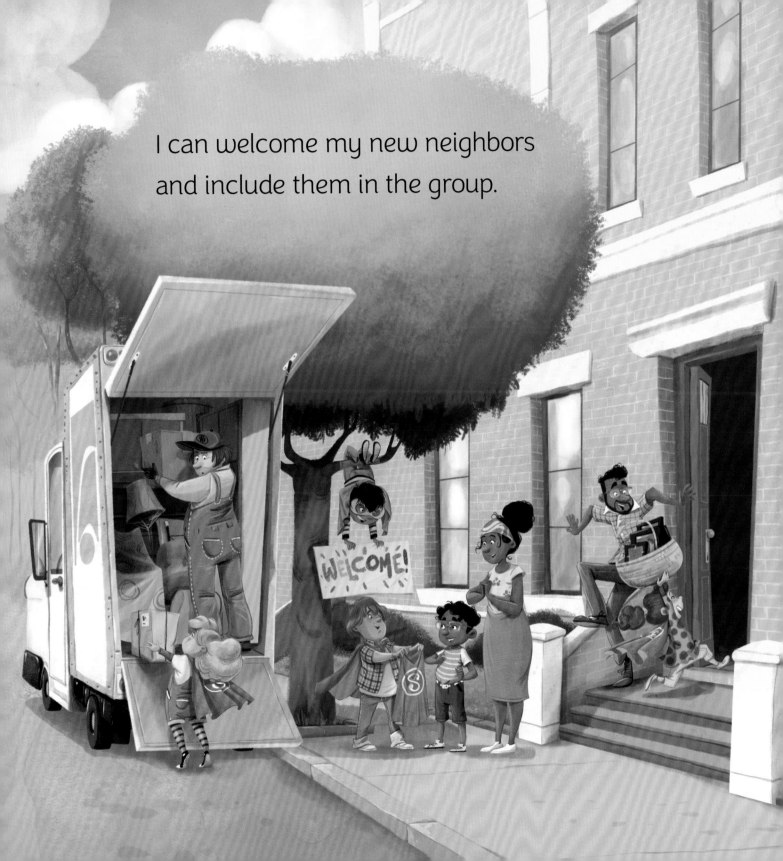

JESUS said to "love each other in the way that I loved you."

Be observant. Be a servant.

Is there something you can do?

Let compassion be your compass.
It will guide you through your days,
show you how to help each other
in the most amazing ways!

If there's something that you notice,
there is something you can do.
Keep your KINDNESS RADAR working—
maybe something
starts with YOU!

One small thing can make a difference.
Let's get started—I can't wait!
All our somethings put together…

will add up to
something great.